JUST DIFFERENT

WRITTEN BY NANCY PETERSON

ILLUSTRATED BY JONATHAN BEISTLINE

CONTENTS

CHAPTER 1

A Summer of Training

The nest hid in the rushes along a far northern lake. A pair of geese watched as tiny cracks appeared in the eggs nestled inside. The eggs rolled about to the music of busy drumming as one by one, the goslings broke free of their bedrooms. The parents honked proudly as they cleaned bits of goo and egg shell off their babies. At last, there was only one egg left.

"Oh dear," said the mother goose, "I am afraid there is something wrong with this one."

However, there was nothing wrong with this last gosling. He had been sound asleep when his brothers and sisters were hatching and had not heard the busy sounds around him. Finally, the baby awoke, and for the first time, he realized that he was quite crowded. How he wanted to stretch his wings! Furiously, he attacked the walls that held him, his little beak tap, tap, tapping until a bit of blue sky appeared. At last, the egg shattered around him and he flopped into a beautiful spring morning.

"Why, he is a fine young flyer," his father crowed. "Look at the length of his wings! We will call this one 'Wilhelm'. Once those breast muscles develop, he will be an awesome flight leader!"

"We will call him Willie," his mother corrected. "He will have to grow into Wilhelm."

❋ ❋ ❋

"Well! Now they are all here, it is time to start training. Goslings! Form a line! No, No, No! A Straight line! You are soldiers! You must have discipline! You are geese, Canada geese! Canada geese are the masters of the sky, the greatest precision flyers since the world began. We earn that title by training. I am your commanding officer. Your mother is my second in command. At all times you will show respect and obey instantly. Your safety, as well as that of the entire gaggle depends on it. Whenever you address us, you will salute. I will now show you the goose salute and you will practice it until you can do it perfectly."

With that, Father Goose stepped forward, puffed out his chest feathers, and smacked his black beak smartly against the front of his neck. The goslings practiced valiantly, but they were still a little unsteady on their webbed feet. Some of them concentrated so hard that they lost their balance and tumbled tail over beak.

It was boot camp from day one. Swimming lessons began immediately. They learned to follow their mother across the lake, perfectly spaced in the pattern their father ordered. They learned to change their configuration smoothly upon command. Once their swimming was flawless, flight school began. Father Goose made them do exercises every day until their breast muscles were strong and their wings well developed. By the time their wing feathers were grown, they were ready to take to the skies. And fly they did! Father Goose taught them to fly in perfect formation, wide vees across the sky. The geese sluiced through the air like a knife. The lead goose met the buffeting wind head on and split it to go around the squadron. It was hard work to be the lead goose, so they learned to take turns, a goose moving into the lead so that the tired goose could drop behind to the end, where the flying was the easiest.

In the afternoons they rested, and fed along the banks where the plants were green and tender. Mother goose taught them to watch out for foxes and coyotes who were always on the lookout for a goose dinner. She taught them how to find the tastiest food and how to sleep with one goose always on guard. They learned that a gaggle was a group of geese and that their highest duty was to the safety of their gaggle. And she told them stories. She talked of the annual Long Flight South and the corn fields rich with plump grain awaiting them at the end of their journey. She spoke of the many gaggle reunions that met at the same place every fall and of the fellowship that kept them busy all winter. She told of the yearning for clear lakes, pine forests, and fresh, cold air that drew them north again each spring. While Father Goose was flying vigilant patrols over the lake, Mother Goose told them that he was the greatest flight commander in the western fly zone. Year after year, his squadron won every flight competition they entered, and he had the best migration safety record of all goose commanders. In a crisis, he was the general they all counted on.

* * *

One day, a few weeks after they were hatched, the goslings heard a noisy commotion approaching from the south.

Startled, the goslings cried, "Mother Goose! What is that?"

As the clamor passed overhead, she sniffed, "Don't worry, dears. Those are Sandhill Cranes, and they are late, as usual. They are the silliest birds ever. It is a wonder they get anywhere at all. Look at them! There is no form. There is no order. They never stop talking and they never even all fly in the same direction, let alone straight! Why, they whirl all over the sky! If most of them are circling to the left, there is at least one joker circling to the right. Your father would have a stroke if he had to migrate with that bunch. He goes out of his way to avoid them."

CHAPTER 2

The Long Flight South

The summer passed pleasantly as summers do, and the goslings lost their downy feathers and grew into strong young geese. As the days shortened, there was urgency to their meals and Mother told them to eat as much as they could to build reserves for the trip ahead. Father Goose became restless and seemed to listen to a call the young geese could not hear.

One day a storm blew in and the geese woke to an inch of snow. It melted quickly, but even the young geese knew a change was coming. That day brought company, and for the first time, the goslings met other geese. Several groups of geese splashed down in their lake and there was excited talk of ice to the north and harvest to the south. Mother Goose explained that these other geese had come to follow their father on the Long Flight South. They all called him General Goose because he was in charge.

At last, the day came and Father Goose called the squadron to attention. "We will leave this morning" he said. "You are all well trained and ready for the journey. It is very important that we stay in formation. We will not fly lower or land until I have thoroughly checked the landscape for danger. Follow all orders instantly, and above all stay together. A lone goose is a cooked goose. Goslings, your mother and I are proud of you. You are now privates of the First Gaggle. It is a pleasure to lead you."

With a rush of wings, the geese took to the skies. They circled once above the lake as if fixing its shape in their minds. Then Father Goose turned south and with a last honk, they were off.

Willie loved to fly, especially when it was his turn to lead. The keen air splint in front of him to rush past his wings. He understood how important it was for the geese behind him to glide in the lee of his wings, each goose lessening the drag for the goose immediately behind. His father always knew when he was getting tired and would give the signal for a change-up. Another goose took his place while Willie dropped back, satisfied with his contribution to the gaggle's flight.

In the evenings Father Goose would sprint ahead to find a safe place for them to land for the night. He knew the route well, and had several alternative landing sites in mind on any given day. One day he led them toward a little lake in the middle of a corn field. The young geese were looking forward to it, because it would be their first taste of corn. Suddenly, Father Goose gave a warning honk and commanded them to wheel toward the left. The gaggle followed orders without question. As they turned in an instant, they heard two loud cracks and the last goose felt something pass behind him. Their training saved his life. The general led them on through the gathering dusk to a lake hidden deep inside a wood.

✳ ✳ ✳

Later, Willie asked, "Sir, what happened back there? What were those noises?"

"Those were gunshots, Willie. A clever hunting blind was hidden in the corn by that lake. Luckily, I saw the sunlight bounce off something shiny and guessed there was danger there. No matter how well you know a place, you must be very cautious when approaching. Our greatest danger from now on will be from hunters and their guns and dogs."

The young geese were subdued that night and knew how lucky they were to have the General for a father.

CHAPTER 3

Disaster

A few days later, they were flying over an area dotted with lakes. The day was overcast and sullen. Without warning, Willie felt himself knocked sideways. An explosion made his ears ring and he began to lose altitude. Instantly, his father was beside him.

"Fly, Willie, fly! Push the air beneath you! Concentrate!"

With great effort Willie began to get some lift, and although his flying was erratic, he stopped his fall. The geese could hear some more shots behind them but they were out of range.

Without leaving Willie's side, Father Goose barked, "Helga, Just to the west of here lies a good sized town with a park in it. There is a large pond at its center. Lead the squadron there and wait until I come. Be careful!"

Flying close to Willie, almost herding him, Father Goose backtracked to a lonely lake in the middle of an abandoned field. Winded and exhausted, Willie touched down with a great splash. Father Goose began a careful inspection. He was relieved to find no blood or broken bones. "Why, Willie, you are a mighty lucky bird! You have lost some flight feathers on your left wing, but they will grow back and the rest of your body is fine."

"But Sir, something is wrong! I can't fly! I can't stay on course!"

"Well, you are rattled, Son. Rest a bit and then we will try again. You are a goose of the First Gaggle, and no goose of the First ever gives up!"

After Willie had rested, the General ordered him into the air. His take- off was awkward at best, but the wounded flyer was airborne. It was then that they both understood the problem. Willie could fly all right but he could only fly in circles. No matter how hard he tried, he could only go round and round, his left wing unable to counter the stroke of the right. At last, discouraged and ashamed, Willie landed on the lake, his father right behind him. In deep thought the commander swam silently around the lake. Miserably, Willie waited for his father's decision. At last, the general paddled back to him.

"Well, Willie, it is pretty clear that you won't be able to migrate with the rest of the squadron. We would make no headway while we waited for you to fly in circles and it would put the whole gaggle in serious jeopardy. It will take a few weeks for those wing feathers to grow in and you are going to have to wait until they do. There is no sense in trying to fly south until you can fly straight. I am going to have to leave you because it is my duty to lead the rest of the gaggle to safety. However, it is still early in the migration season and there will be plenty of other geese coming through. Whenever you see a gaggle approaching, give the goose distress call three times. It is part of the goose oath for any goose to come to the aid of another when that call is heard. The squadron leader will help you try a test flight. As soon as you can fly straight, come south with that gaggle. Tell the leader you are my son and he will know how to find us."

"Yes, Sir,", Willie muttered, terrified at the thought of staying behind alone.

His father added, "Whatever you do, do not try to fly south by yourself. Remember, a lone goose is a cooked goose. Also, never, ever go to sleep at the edge of the lake. When you are tired, sleep in the middle of the lake where no predator can reach you. Be alert when you feed along the banks, and always be ready for an ambush. You can't be too careful! Do exercises every day to keep that wing in shape. Son, you are a soldier of the First Gaggle. You are a valiant Canada Goose and you will make your mother proud!"

The General made him practice the distress call until he was sure that Willie could do it well. Then, Father Goose gave his son a smart salute. Willie returned it and watched the general take off. As he watched his father fly out of sight, the lump in Willie's throat felt as big as the egg from which he had hatched.

❊ ❊ ❊

The lake was cold and its banks unfriendly. Willie had never felt so lonely or afraid. He spent the days peering at the sky, hoping to spot some geese. Every few days another gaggle flew over. Willie would give the special distress call, and sure enough the geese would land. Each time, Willie would labor into the air with the squadron leader. Each time, in spite of his best efforts, Willie flew in circles, and each time, the leader shook his head. "Sorry, soldier. If you can't fly straight, you can't fly with us." Wishing him luck, the geese continued on their way, leaving Willie discouraged and feeling lonelier than ever.

The days grew into weeks and Willie still couldn't fly straight. The time between gaggles grew longer, and Willie began to worry that the migration was over and he had missed all of the chances to head south. The lake started to freeze at night and he was concerned that one morning he would wake up and find himself trapped in the ice. The food wasn't all that good, and he wondered if he would starve.

One grey, drizzly day Willie hit rock bottom. He hadn't seen any geese in over a week, and as far as he could tell, his wing feathers still weren't long enough to change the way he flew. He had been unable to sleep the night before because the wind had turned the lake into a dizzying ride of cold waves that threatened to throw him against the banks. He tried to nibble at the old, dead grass, but he was so tired he kept drifting off to sleep. Vaguely he remembered his father telling him not to sleep along the bank, but he decided not to worry this once. Tucking his head beneath his wings, Willie fell sound asleep among the cat tails, gently rocked by the lapping waves.

CHAPTER 4

Rescue

Willie woke to such a ruckus that he started to fly before his wings were even spread. Out of the corner of his eye, he caught a glimpse of a bushy tailed fox beating a hasty retreat. Willie was surrounded by sandhill cranes. There must have been three hundred birds in the water around him, all beating their wings and splashing water so that it felt like he was in the middle of a fountain. And the noise! They were all squawking loudly, completely out of tune and without unison.

At last, the crane who seemed to be their leader started yelling over the din. "Quiet! Quiet! Pipe down fer Pete's sake!" The cranes quieted down enough that the leader could make himself heard. "Well, young feller, whatcha' doin' out here all by yerself? Ya came purty close to bein' the guest of honor at the fox convention. Ol' Sly Fox was one jump away from baggin' ya when we dropped in on the party. By the way, my name's Sam, and I'm the dude in charge of this band of hooligans. About all that means is that I get to pick the general direction we're goin' for the day.

We're purty much free spirits, so it's anybody's guess where we'll end up for the night."

"Thank you for saving me, Sir," Willie stuttered. My name is Willie, and well, I'm here because I can't fly straight, so I can't fly with anybody else."

Sam hollered, "I can't hear what this young feller's saying, so shut up!" He looked at Willie. "Now what did ya say the trouble was?"

"I can't fly straight!" Willie yelled. "My wing is damaged and I can only fly in circles, so I can't fly with anybody! I have to wait until I can fly straight before I make the Long Flight South."

Sam looked puzzled. "But…ya can fly, right?"

"Yes, Sir, but only in circles so I have to wait here, and I can't go alone because my father says a lone goose is a cooked goose."

"Don't call me sir! My name is Sam! Ya make me sound like that stuffed shirt general of a Canada goose. Say, there's a feller with no sense of humor! Now, explain to me again what the problem is? If ya can fly, what's keepin' ya here? Don't ya know yer gonna get frozen in one fine night, and that fox'll be able to skate right to ya fer a goose dinner on ice?"

"Don't you understand?" Willie beat his wings up and down in frustration. "I can only fly in circles!"

"So?" Sam shrugged his wings. "Why is that a problem? I mean, it's way more fun to fly that way."

"Well, how do you get anywhere?" Willie asked, curious in spite of himself.

"Tell ya what, young feller! Whyn't ya come with us and we'll show ya. It's as easy as pie! Ya really shouldn't stay here and yer kind is pretty well cleared out north a here. We haven't seen any Canada geese in a couple a weeks."

Willie didn't know what to do. He remembered his mother telling him how crazy Sandhill Cranes were, but he also knew Sam was right. He decided to give it a try. If he couldn't keep up or started causing collisions, he could always land on another lake. Willie nodded his head in agreement.

CHAPTER 5

Flying in Circles

"**G**ood job, Feller! We'll be glad to have yer company!" Sam whacked Willie on his back with his wing. 'hey! Listen up, Guys!" The squawking died down to a dull roar. "This here is Willie. He's sort a down to one wing right now, so he's comin' with us. He can only go in one direction for the time bein', so that means he's gonna get to be 'it' at least half the time. But that's okay, him bein' a guest n' all. We'll probably have to explain the game to him, him bein' a Canada Goose. I swear, them fellers don't know much about havin' fun!"

The rest of the cranes yelled and whooped, and several of the younger ones tried to put him up on their shoulders. Willie felt dazed and more than a little frightened, but what else could he do?

After much hubbub, Sam got several of the older cranes lined up to help Willie "find the up draft", whatever that meant. With a great whirring of wings, the cranes stopped milling about long enough to take off. In spite of the fact that the cranes looked exceedingly awkward as they left the ground, Willie was impressed with the tremendous rush of upward air that carried them all into the sky. Instead of leveling off the way geese do, the cranes continued their upward thrust, higher than Willie had ever been. Suddenly, Willie realized, that although he was still struggling mightily to make his left wing beat as hard as his right, the birds around him were hardly moving.

"Why don't cha lean back and relax, young feller?" Sam was gliding right next to him. "Let the wind do the work. It's goin' the same way we want to, more or less."

Willie was stunned. He stopped beating his wings, although he held them ready to take over when he stalled and began falling. By golly! He felt himself pushed by a lazy current that held his body in the air, almost as if he were floating gently on a lake. Experimenting carefully, he discovered that he could change his direction with small adjustments of his wings. He noticed that the entire flock was flowing in a wide circle that meandered south, even though the birds were hardly doing any work at all. This was fun! At first, he spent his time looking at the ground, realizing that when he had been part of the gaggle, he had been concentrating so hard on flying in formation that he had hardly noticed what passed below. The land was beautiful, and there was so much to see! He began to have an appreciation for how much knowledge his father had.

Willie also began to understand why Sandhill cranes made so much noise during their migrations. They never stopped talking! Someone was always telling a story or a joke, and they laughed even at the lame ones. The younger ones were constantly play-ing tricks on one another or trying to talk Sam into landing for a bite to eat. He was good natured about it, but Willie realized that Sam was the leader, for he kept them flowing south without being bossy about it.

By the third day, Sam decided that Willie had caught the hang of riding the air waves and gave the cranes permission to teach him how to play "bumps". This game involved picking someone to be "it" who then circled the opposite way from the direction all the rest were going, the object being to dodge everyone else.

The first bird to bump into him won the round and got to be "it" next. The first few times he played, Willie was scared to death, but thanks to all the exercises and training he did under his father's watchful eye, Willie got to be quite good at the game and was very popular with the young cranes.

One day, Willie saw what could only be a hunting blind. There were several humans dressed in orange around it. He nearly panicked and quickly caught up with Sam. "There are hunters down there, Sam. Shouldn't we try to evade them?"

"What fer?" Sam said. They never bother us cranes. Fer one thing, we're as tough and stringy as old dead cats, and fer another, it's against their law to shoot at us. I don't think they would look fer a goose up here with us, so keep yer feathers on."

CHAPTER 6

The Son of Stuffed Shirt

As the days wore by, Willie started noticing Canada geese floating on the lakes below. Although it was fun to fly with the cranes, he suddenly felt homesick for his family. About then, Sam dropped back to fly beside him. "Willie, who did ya say was yer kin?"

"What? Oh, you mean my family!" Willie's eyes began to glow. "Well, sir…I mean Sam, my father is the commander of the First Gaggle. Everyone says he is the greatest leader in the entire western fly zone, and all the geese call him 'General'."

Sam about did a back flip. "Ya mean to say yer pa is the ol' stuffed bird hisself?! Well, I'll be derned! I never would'a thunk it, considerin' how nice ya are to get along with, an' all!"

Willie shook himself indignantly. "Sam, my father is wonderful! He is smart and brave and a great teacher, and…and…"

"Now, now, keep yer feathers on." Sam soothed. "Yer right, I don't know the bird maself, an' maybe he ain't so bad as we hear. Guess we get all het up cause' a what we hear he says about us cranes. Sorry if I got ya upset."

"That's okay," Willie replied. "I forgive you." But do you know where his gaggle might be? I've been thinking that I should drop out and start asking some of the other geese how to find him."

"No need fer that, young feller, Sam assured. "Everybody on this ol' flyway knows where he hangs out. That goose has staked out the best corn fields in three states fer his flock to winter."

"It is called a gaggle, not a flock, Sam." Willie corrected

"Whatever. The deal is there is a great big lake completely sur-rounded by corn fields, and it belongs to some human who really likes us birds so he don't let no hunters on and he leaves strips of corn fer us to munch on all winter. The only problem is, yer dad drives all the rest of us off, which an't real neighborly, if ya catch my drift."

Willie was confused, caught in the middle between his father and his new friends. "Well, maybe I could talk to him and tell him how nice you are, because, really, I don't think he has ever talked to a crane before. All of the geese just think they know about you, and they have all sorts of opinions that aren't true at all."

"Well, young feller, if ya can make a difference, well, I'd be purty surprised, but I'd be grateful, too. Yer dad's outfit is coming up on the left there. See that lake and look at them cornfields! We jest might hang around an extry day or two jest to see if ya can make any headway with her pa. Thanks fer flying with us. It's been a mighty pleasure. Guess you helped me think about geese a little different, too."

"Thank you, Sam! Thank you for saving my life! Twice! If you hadn't helped me fly south with you, I'd probably be dead by now. Good bye everyone! Thanks for teaching me how to play Bumps!"

CHAPTER 7

The Difference

Amid a noisy chorus of good byes, Willie dropped below the flock of cranes and drifted down to the lake. To his joy, he found that he could almost fly straight now and would not be embarrassed to fly in front of the gaggle. He saw his family on the far side of the lake and descended right in the middle of them.

"My gosh! Willie! Helga, it's Willie!" His father raced to him and wrapped his neck around Willie's. Everyone crowded around him, all asking questions at once. They reminded Willie of the cranes for a short minute, until the General roared, "Attention! Silence!" The noise shut off as if a valve had been turned.

"No", Willie thought. "Not like the cranes at all."

"How did you get here, Son? The last gaggle of geese came by last week and said you were still not ready. They didn't think there were any geese behind them. I had given up hope."

"I didn't come with geese, Da…I mean Sir. I flew with a flock of Sandhill cranes."

"OH NO!" his mother wailed. My poor son! It must have been terrible!"

"No, Mother. It was fine. In fact, it was a lot of fun, and I learned a whole lot that I would have never known if I hadn't gone with them. Sir, they saved my life." Willie told them about the fox and how the cranes offered to make the Long Flight South with him, even if he couldn't fly straight.

The general was silent for a long while. "Obviously," he muttered. "I've been very wrong about the cranes. It just goes to show, a goose should never believe everything he hears without searching for the truth himself. They are noisy buggers though, and I don't care what you say, they are not organized!"

Willie nodded in agreement, then added timidly, "Sir? The guys in Sam's flock are really good birds even if they do approach life differently. And…well, they think it is unfair of you not to share these fields with them. Do you think it would be all right if they wintered here, too?"

Willie heard one of the older geese mumble, "There goes the neighborhood."

The General turned on him in a flash. "What did you say, Captain?" Speak up! Remember, these cranes brought my son safely south when a hundred flights of geese, including mine, would not! Willie, Swim with me a while and tell me what you learned."

CHAPTER 8

The Order of the Tin Goose

The general and Willie made a slow tour around the lake while his father peppered him with questions. "You say, you could see the route really well while you were in these wind currents?" he asked. And are you sure hunters don't shoot at cranes?"

"All I can tell you, Sir, is that we flew right over the top of a dozen hunting blinds and I never heard a single bang. "

"Do you think Sam would let you fly with his flock sometimes so you could scout out the way?"

Willie nodded his head excitedly.

"Would you be willing to do some special operations, some spying for us? It might be dangerous because you would have to fly back alone to warn us if something was wrong."

"Yes, Sir! I could do it easily, and I don't think it would be too dangerous because the cranes taught me to fly really high. They ride up-drafts so high it almost makes you dizzy."

"Please don't tell your mother that," the general said dryly.

❋ ❋ ❋

That afternoon, the General called a special meeting. All of the geese stood at attention. "Private Wilhelm, please step forward. You are now promoted to the rank of lieutenant. Also, in recognition of courage and decisive action under extreme circumstances, I hereby award you the Order of the Tin Goose, the highest honor in the land."

Willie privately thought the whole thing was blown out of proportion and that if any one deserved a medal, it was Sam. However, he politely thanked the geese and accepted their congratulations.

"Furthermore," the General added, "I intend to issue an invitation to the flock of Sandhill cranes under the command of one Sam... I'm sorry, I don't know his rank...to winter in the cornfield nearest the farmer's home. Lieutenant Wilhelm, it shall be your first duty to take this invitation to Sam and to arrange for us to meet."

"Sir, Sam doesn't have a rank, but I'll be glad to give him your message." Said Willie.

That night Willie went to sleep as happy as the day he hatched. He was so glad his father understood. Sandhill Cranes weren't silly or stupid. They were just different.

About the Author

Nancy Peterson

Nan grew up on a cattle ranch in the Colorado mountains, became a practicing large animal veterinarian, and operates a cattle ranch in the Nebraska Sandhills. She and her husband have three grown children and several grandchildren. This book was inspired by the annual sandhill crane migration over her ranch and was born from her life-long love of nature, wide open spaces, and storytelling.

About the Illustrator

Jonathan Beistline

Jonathan draws out of Northern Colorado with his wife and three children. The illustrations in this book are done with ink and wash and showcases Jonathan's love of gesture drawing from nature, on-location, and from observation.